Wilhelm Hauff

The Wine-Ghosts of Bremen

Wilhelm Hauff

The Wine-Ghosts of Bremen

1st Edition | ISBN: 978-3-75237-798-9

Place of Publication: Frankfurt am Main, Germany

Year of Publication: 2020

Outlook Verlag GmbH, Germany.

Reproduction of the original.

THE

WINE-GHOSTS OF BREMEN

BY

WILHELM HAUFF

PREFACE.

When Mr. Carlyle endeavoured to introduce Jean Paul Richter to the English public, it seems to us that he was more than usually unsuccessful. The literary publics of the England and the Germany of those days were very different, and perhaps the errors of taste, which each professed to find in the other, were not in truth wholly upon the side of John Bull. We feel, (with much deprecation of our own impudence in challenging such a comparison,) in a somewhat similar position, and dread in our more diffident moments a far colder reception and far greater depth of oblivion for our present attempt to render into English a good German story about STRONG DRINK. German humour is often more rollicking than that of our own countrymen; it is also occasionally more subtle. But it has always been a matter of some wonder to us that Hauff's acknowledged masterpiece should be unknown to English readers, and we have therefore made the following attempt; praying the courteous reader only that he will not throw the story down in disgust till he gets to the best part: of the location of which we allow him to be the best judge.

Wilhelm Hauff was born on the 29th November, 1802, at Stuttgart, where his father held various high posts, with various high-sounding double and treble official names, under the paternal government of the Elector Frederick, the first of his name and house who attained 'serenity.' It was this same ruler who three years later, after refusing a passage to Napoleon's troops for some time with great show of patriotism, allowed himself to be 'convinced,' as soon as the Emperor himself appeared and offered him a considerable extension of territory and a Royal Crown; and who confessed with some *naïveté* 'that since Frederick the Great he had never met any one so good at talking a man over as Napoleon; that the latter had in fact the same "tournure de l'esprit" as Frederick.' But His Serene Highness was, in common with many of his contemporaries, in the habit of allowing himself to be talked over by any one with a good strong army at his back. 'C'était leur nature de complaire aux plus forts.' Therefore he now openly joined, in 1805, as he had practically done in '95 and '99, the row of princely traitors to the cause of Germany, and began to dance with his fellows on the fast-closing grave of the Holy Roman Empire. It must however be remembered that his country was one of the few German principalities that still possessed an active 'Landstände' or system of Estates: this was indeed of the most rudimentary order, and consisted chiefly of representatives of the nobles, craft gilds, and ecclesiastical corporations; but it is worthy of note that, as in the Tyrol, there was a Peasants' Estate in Württemberg, and that these Estates did possess, though they rarely made good, the right of voting or withholding supplies from His Serenity. On the occasion referred to, when he expressed some doubts as to whether his Estates would agree to the proposed treaty, Napoleon, who had methods of his own for dealing with refractory representatives, answered that 'he would settle all that.' The Elector then got his crown from Napoleon; but in November, 1813, a very similar scene was enacted at Stuttgart, (with Alexander in place of Napoleon,) when the confederation of the Rhine was dissolved, and Bavaria had already made her peace with the allies by the treaty of Ried. Then the magnanimous King Frederick threw in his lot with the winning side again, in return for that fatal guarantee of absolute sovereignty and territorial indemnification for his losses, (for he was obliged to disgorge some of the spoils of his neighbours,) which proved such an obstacle in the way of the long-deferred restoration of Germany.

Growing up under influences like these, it is wonderful that young Hauff and his brother Hermann (his senior by two years) should ever have discovered that they were Germans at all; but they lost their father in 1809 and do not afterwards appear to have had any political connection with the government: and by 1815, when Wilhelm was only thirteen, the worst was over and the people of Stuttgart were left face to face with their amiable monarch; who surprised them and all the world by granting them of his own grace and favour an absolutely free constitution. This, however, on the principle of 'Timeo Danaos et dona ferentes,' was too much for the Württembergers, who profoundly mistrusted him: but before the matter could be settled King Frederick died, and King Wilhelm I, the husband of a Russian princess, and a brave soldier and able diplomatist, who had stood up for the rights of Germany in the deferred Elsass question, gave to his people, after much preparation, a very respectably constitutional form of government with two chambers, which included a representation both of clergy and old-imperial nobility, backed up by a strong Executive. This was in 1822, and the remaining five years of W. Hauff's life were passed in a happy country that had no history. It is usual of course to account for the excessively fertile development of literary culture in Germany at this time by the fact that the system of repression was so strong and effective as to drive all the moderate minds away from politics; but this will hardly hold good in Württemberg. Yet the educated classes there seem to have been completely indifferent to such politics as there were. But there were very few.

Those who want to discover the conditions under which Hauff's earlier life passed should read (1) Goethe's Autobiography in Wahrheit and Dichtung, and (2) Histoire d'un Conscrit; and, by mixing the two well together, may arrive at some sort of idea what life was like in a small German state, on which were grafted the new horrors of a military despotism. It is not a pleasant picture, but if it bred a good many souls as dead to patriotism as Goethe's and Heine's, it also bred not a few Müllers and Uhlands and Arndts; and it bred Wilhelm Hauff. That Hauff, in his later years at least (if a man can be said to have later years who died at twenty-five), had caught much of the spirit of the heroes of the War of Liberation, is best seen from the few soul-stirring lyrics which he has left, especially the two odes which he wrote in 1823-4 on the anniversary of the battle of Waterloo; even more perhaps it is seen in his admiration for W. Müller, and in the affecting story that when on his deathbed he heard the news of the battle of Navarino, he cried, 'What news! I must go hence and tell it to Müller,' who preceded him to the grave by a few weeks.

Hauff and his brother were voracious readers. Their maternal grandfather, 'a learned jurist,' (one trembles to think what a learned German jurist must have been like in the first decade of this century,) had a good library, consisting chiefly of old Law and History books, but including also a considerable number of romances; 'Smollett, Fielding, and Goldsmith were there,' says his biographer, Gustav Schwab, in the life which he prefixed to the 1837 (first collected) edition of Hauff's works. Schwab relates, not without humour, how the boys would play at fortress building and sieges with some of the more ponderous of the volumes, and the delight which they took in battering down a breastwork composed of the 'Acta Pacis Westphalicæ,' perhaps at the very time at which the Congress of Vienna was engaged upon the same job. But in the way of reading, they battened chiefly upon the old German historical romances, Hardleder's 'Ursache des Deutschen Krieges' especially, and it was from works like these that Wilhelm caught that old-imperial swing and flow of ideas which carries us so powerfully through Lichtenstein and the 'Phantasien.' The plan of turning a boy loose in a library is sometimes justified by results, although not always in the way expected. But although Wilhelm got a certain amount of classics drilled into him at the cloister school of Blaubeuern, and afterwards studied 'Philology, Philosophy, and Theology,' from 1820-1824, at the University of Tübingen, 'more,' says Schwab, 'to please his mother than from any leaning of his own to those subjects,' he never could write Greek or Latin verses like his brother, or pass for anything but an essentially poor scholar. But several other people who have afforded some pleasure to the world at large have been essentially poor scholars.

This deficiency did not affect him much; his mother, though apparently not wealthy, had good interest, and procured for him, when he left the University, the position of private tutor in the family of 'the at that time War's-council's-President, later War's-minister von Hügel' at Stuttgart, where he remained two years, with apparently abundant leisure for exercising his talent for writing poetical romances and fairy tales, of which during the last two years of his life he poured forth an incessant stream. It is worth while noting that in one of these—the first part of the 'Memoirs of Satan' (not the completed edition of these memoirs as they now stand)—is a passage in which the author falls foul of the great Autocrat of German Literature apropos of some lines in Faust; which was a more daring thing for a young fellow of four-and-twenty to do than it is possible for a man living in a free country to imagine. The rash youth afterwards repented, and expunged the obnoxious passage when he finished the memoirs of his black Majesty.

Perhaps it would have been as well if there had been no expunging, at least we may dare to say so on this side of the water, where less and less divinity hedges the person of the great man-god of letters every day. Hauff, however, had a tender heart, and did not like to see what a big hole he had made by casting a stone at the man-god; and with the modesty of twenty-four he begged pardon. History does not say whether the man-god took any notice of him.

It is not, however, with the Memoirs of Satan, or with any but one of Hauff's works that we are now concerned. The 'Man in the Moon' was a scathing satire upon a school of story-book makers, popular at the time, and headed by one H. von Clauren, whose works we have not perused. 'Lichtenstein,' which has been dramatised, is not inferior to an inferior Waverley novel. These and many more are well known to English readers, but the 'Phantasien im Bremer Rathskeller' has never been translated, no doubt because of its dreadfully Rabelaisian morality in the matter of strong drink. What can you think of a man who dedicates his book to the 'lovers of wine,' and takes for his motto the passage from Othello which appears at the head of the story? We do not intend to defend him; we ourselves are by no means the pair of ultra-Pickwickian topers, that a cursory perusal of the motto and dedication would lead the reader to believe: and we are quite aware that there *are* to be no more cakes and ale in this world; we are a little sorry for it, that is all. As for Hauff we will let him speak for himself; we have no reason whatever to believe that he had more than a poetical and literary affection for the juice of the grape.

Hauff had grown tired of being a private tutor in 1826, and spent the profits of Lichtenstein in a journey to the North of Germany and to Paris in the latter half of that year. It was upon that occasion that he visited Bremen, although not upon the errand imagined in the text. On his return to the South in 1827 he became Editor of the 'Morning News for the Educated Classes,' to which his brother, who succeeded him in the editorship, was already a contributor. This paper survived till 1865, when it expired a few months after the death of Hermann Hauff, whom from all we know of him we imagine to have been a much more business-like editor than Wilhelm. Contemporarily with this responsible post Wilhelm took to himself a wife, one of his own cousins, who bore him a daughter but a few days before his death. He died of fever on the 18th November, 1827. Prefixed to the edition of 1853 is a very pretty little poem of L. Uhland's on the occasion, and also a funeral oration by Mr. Court Chaplain Grüneisen, who was his cousin, both of which were recited over his grave in true German fashion. If we could believe all that this worthy priest said—and we have not a scrap of evidence to the contrary—Wilhelm Hauff's life must indeed have been a bright and happy one; 'Wonnezeit voll holder Träume,' as he himself called the season of youth. Apparently he made no enemies, and he made every one whom he chose his friend; his tender affection for his mother seems to have been the mainspring of his existence; to his bride he had been long attached in a half playful spirit, that wanted only the shadow of a difficulty to withdraw their love into those regions of romance in which his mind delighted to dwell. It was about a month before his death that he produced, as a reminiscence of his northern journey, the following story, entitled—

'THE WINE-GHOSTS OF BREMEN.'

NOTE (*written before the late incorporation of the Hanse towns with the Empire*).

It may seem a little superfluous here to attempt to describe the Rathskeller at Bremen, for it is well known to many travellers. But from the method by which travellers are usually conducted through the vaults, in which Hauff spent his grandfather's *Schalttag* in that bygone October, little acquaintance with the object of his story is to be derived. The Rathhaus at Bremen, then, is by far the most conspicuous object in the town. It contains some of the most beautiful of the German efforts, both in stone and wood carving, of the fifteenth and sixteenth centuries. Whether there is any connection between the fact that the fifteenth century preferred stone, the sixteenth wood, and the other fact that the former of these centuries was to the Hanse towns the epoch of glory, the latter the epoch of decay, we must leave for Mr. Ruskin to decide. Anyhow, the men who embellished that Rathhaus inside were as little conscious of the decay of their city as those who built it and decorated it outside. So far as Germany is concerned, even in the best examples of Lübeck, Augsburg, or Nuremberg, the force of Art could no further go. But descend the steps on the left of the building, and you will find a very different state of things. The cellar is built as a cellar should be, strictly with a view to the practical—that is, to the comfort of its inhabitants, the mighty spirits imprisoned in the mighty casks. For the comfort of those who came to commune with those mighty spirits, a broad oak settle with strong arms would and did suffice; and the steps were made strictly with a view to be *easy of ascent*. Since Hauff's time, and partly in consequence of his story, the internal arrangements appear to have been much altered. Some of the cellar chambers have been painted in the true modern German style, about which we should prefer not to say too much. Some of the mural paintings profess to be representations of scenes in the story. There is no longer a passage straight through from the Apostle cellar to the boudoir of Frau Rosa herself, and of the other vaults the cellar of Bacchus is alone unaltered. Bacchus, indeed, is the hero of the place. No better description could possibly be given of him than that which Hauff gives, and therefore we will not attempt to amplify it. But the same Bacchus does not actually 'in the wood,' so to speak, sit there. He was taken down ten years ago, and a new one put up in his place—why, I failed to discover. His cask is, however, like all the other casks except Frau Rosa (who has disappeared altogether), the old one, a veritable Thirty Years War cask, beautifully carved with fantastic figures in relief. In the Apostle cellar all the wine is Hochheimer or Rüdesheimer, and the names are still graven on each cask, and 'Herr Judas, 1729,' is said to contain the best wine. But from a somewhat limited experience it is difficult cordially to endorse the reported opinion of the late King Ludwig of Bavaria, that the finest Rhine wines would keep for ever. Let the man who wishes to know what wine *can be*, by all means go daily for a few weeks to the Rathskeller in Bremen. Let him pay due homage to the worthies of old time there by tasting them, one glass of each per diem; but let him not fail to wash them down speedily with a bottle of twenty-year old Niersteiner or Rüdesheimer. If you ask, thirsty reader, why these things are to be found at their best in Bremen, we can only say that North Germany is a right conservative country; and because the Burgomasters of Bremen thought it their duty in the seventeenth century to lay down cask upon cask of the best vintages, their successors think it is their duty likewise; which is a very practical and righteous feeling. Bacchus, however, and the two mighty casks which guard his right hand and his left (like those trusty comrades who stand up in the halls of the Colleges of our Universities on each side of the drinker, when the loving cup is passed round, to prevent his being stabbed in the back), are now empty. The right hand cask was broken open and drained by the French soldiers in 1806, after the defeat of Prussia at Auerstädt; a loss which one can well imagine that the Town Council of Bremen bore less philosophically than many another act of power of those merciless freebooters. Bacchus himself, who dates from 1624, has been empty for 100 years. But what has become of the Rose herself? There are many old casks in the cellar called after her, but none that I could identify with the heroine of the story. She is still painted on the ceiling—a sufficiently ugly specimen (of the variety known as 'La France,' she appears to be)—very fat and round, with very dirty green foliage, and round her the following inscription:—

'Cur Rosa Flos Veneris Bacchi depingitur antro,

Causa quod absque mero frigiat ipsa Venus.'

Other bad hexameters follow in other parts of the vault known as the Rose cellar; as for instance:

'Haec Rosa Luminibus Veneres Nectarque Palato

Objicit, exhalans pocula grata cadis:

Vina vetusta tenet, grandævi munera Bacchi;

Sint procul hinc juvenes; vos decet iste senes.'

They are in fact the sort of verses that the traditional Eton boy, who wrote verses for the whole of his Dame's house, could turn out at the rate of a couplet a minute, adding a few false quantities and concords by desire of the accomplice for whom they were written, 'because if you don't, you know, my tutor will never believe they're my own composition.' Finally, over the entrance door, on the other side of which is a medallion of Hauff, erected in 1876, comes the following:—

'Was Magen, Leib und Herz, Saft, Kraft, und Geist kann geben,

Betrübte trösten mag, halbtodte kann beleben,

Theilt diese Rose mit, sie hat von hundert Jahren

Den Preis ein edles Oel mit Sorgfalt zu bewahren.'

More could be quoted, but this breathes the spirit of the eighteenth century quite sufficiently for our purpose.

As for Roland, he is still in the marketplace, a wonderful fourteenth-century stone figure, nearly twenty feet high, not standing on a pillar, but simply on a pedestal about two feet from the ground. He would certainly find it remarkably difficult to sit down, even on a cask, for he has iron spikes to his knees, which would make him extremely uncomfortable if he bent them. He did not bow his head to me as I went away as he did to Hauff, which I felt deeply. It is generally believed that he only bows his head to those departing visitors who have had enough Nierstein to appreciate the compliment.

C. R. L. F.

THE WINE-GHOSTS OF BREMEN.

'Come, come, good wine is a good familiar creature if it be well used.'—
Othello, ii. 3.

'There's nothing to be done with the fellow,' I heard them say, as they
stumped down the stairs; 'nine o'clock and he is going to doze away his
evening like a dormouse. He wouldn't have been like that four years ago.'
They were not far wrong from their point of view, good fellows; for this
evening there was to be a most brilliant musical tea and muffin fight with
dancing and recitation, and these gentlemen had come to invite me (who was
a stranger to the High Life of Bremen) to go with them. But I did not feel up
to it. Some one, whom I had come to Bremen on purpose to visit, was not to
be there, and what's the use of going anywhere where Some one isn't?
Besides, I knew I should have to sing if I went, and I didn't choose to sing if
she wasn't to be there to hear me. I should only spoil all their fun by looking
sulky. I preferred to let them curse me for a dull dog for a few minutes on the
steps, rather than let them bore themselves from nine to one in talking to my
body only, while my soul would be whole streets off wandering about in the
neighbourhood of the Frauenkirche.

It wasn't sleepiness though. I am not a habitual dormouse, and don't like
being called one. No, I meant to be thoroughly awake that night, and one of
my friends—it was you, Hermann—said as much when he got outside. 'He
didn't look sleepy,' I heard him say, 'with those bright eyes of his. But he
looked like a man who had been drinking either too much or too little, which
probably means that he is going to make a night of it with the bottle, and
alone.'

Prophetic soul! Did you know that my eyes were sparkling yet
proleptically with the thought of old Rhenish? You didn't know that I had a
permit from their High Mightinesses to greet my Lady Rose and the Twelve
Apostles. And you certainly didn't know that it was my 'Retreat.'[1]

In my opinion the habit which I inherit from my grandfather of blazing, so
to speak, the tree of life here and there with a notch, and spending a quiet day
of meditation over each notch, is not a bad one. To keep the ordinary festivals

9

of the Church only is hardly sufficient; one becomes commonplace, and one's thoughts are too apt to become commonplace on such days. But let the soul that keeps an anniversary of its own making keep it alone; look inwards for a few hours in the year instead of always outwards; sit down at the long table d'hôte of memory, people it with the shadows of the past, and then set to and make out the bill conscientiously. Such days as these my grandfather always kept, and called his 'retreats.' He didn't prepare a banquet for his friends, or pass the time in festivity at all; he simply sat down and feasted his own soul and talked to her in that inner chamber which she had occupied for five-and-seventy years. Even now I can trace, long as it is since the dear old man was laid in the churchyard, the marked passages in his Elzevir Horace which he always read on such days; and as I read, I can see his large blue eyes wandering thoughtfully over the yellow leaves of memory's book. He takes up his pen. Slowly and hesitatingly he draws the black cross beneath the name of some dear departed friend. 'The master is keeping his Retreat,' whispered the servants to us, as we grandchildren were running gaily and noisily up the stairs; and we repeated the words to each other, and imagined that he was making himself Christmas presents, and wondered how he managed to light up his own Christmas tree. And we were not far wrong. They were the tapers of affection that he was kindling upon the tree of Unforgetfulness, each taper the symbol of happy hours of a long life. And when his hours of solitude were passed, and we were admitted in the evening, he sat still and quiet in his chair as if he rejoiced like a child in the Heaven-sent Christmas gifts of the past.

And it was on his Retreat day that he was borne by loving hands to his last resting-place. For the first time for many years, (for he had been confined to his room,) it was 'out into the air,' but it was also 'into his grave.' And again, 'I could not choose but weep they should lay him in the mould.' I had often walked with him along the same road; but when they turned off across the black bridge and laid him deep in the earth, I knew that he was keeping his real Retreat. I was a little boy, and I wondered as they threw a lot of stones and turf on him whether he would ever come up again. He did not. But his image remained in my memory, and when I grew up my favourite pieces in the long picture-gallery of Reflection were his Retreats.

And isn't to-day mine? The First of September? And am I to go and drink weak tea and listen to bad music to-day? No! I have a better prescription in my pocket, directed to the best apothecary in the world—somewhat under the world in fact he dwells. Down therefore to him, and *Fiat, sum., haust. ad lib.*

It was striking ten o'clock when I descended the broad steps that lead to the noble vault, which with all its contents is the ancient and perpetual inheritance of their High Mightinesses the Corporation of Bremen. There was every probability of my having my drink to myself, as there was a fearful storm raging outside and no one about in the streets. The cellarman stared at me as I presented a slip of paper, signed and sealed by a town-councillor:—

'Admit the Bearer to Drink. Sep. 1st.'

'So late and *To-night*?' says he. 'It is never late before twelve and never too early after that for good wine,' says I. He looked at the signature and seal, and not without hesitation led the way through the vaults. What a noble sight was there! His lantern shone over long rows of casks, and threw strange forms and shadows on the arches of the cellar; and the pillars seemed to float in the background like busy coopers plying their staves. My companion wanted to open for me one of those smaller rooms where six or eight friends at the most can pack in with comfortable space to let the bottle circulate: and a very proper thing it is, when your companions are the right sort, to sit close together; but when I am to be alone I love free space, where my thoughts and my body can find room to expand. So I chose an old vaulted hall, the largest we passed into, for my solitary banquet-room. 'You expect company?' said the attendant. 'No.' Some have who do not expect,' said he, with an uneasy glance at the shadow on the wall. 'What do you mean?'

'Nothing. It's the first of September.... By-the-bye, there was Mr. Councillor Pumpernickel here a while agone, and he bade me get out some samples for you—samples of my Lady Rose and of the Twelve Apostle casks'; and he began to take down some pretty little bottles with long strips of paper on their necks. 'You don't mean to tell me I am not to be allowed to drink out of the casks themselves.' 'Your honour couldn't possibly be allowed that privilege except in the presence of a town-councillor. Let me fill your honour's glass from this bottle.' 'Not a drop here then,' said I; 'if I mayn't drink from the cask head I will drink at the cask side at least. Come, old fellow, pick up your samples, and give me the light.' He still kept fidgeting about, and shoving the bottles into and out of his pockets, which irritated me much, as I was longing to be off to the Apostle cellar; and at length I spoke quite sharply, 'Come now, march.' This gave him courage apparently, and he answered with some firmness, 'It won't do, sir, really it won't—not to-night.' Thinking he was merely angling to raise his price, I pressed a substantial douceur into his hand, and took him by the arm to lead him along. 'No, no, it wasn't that I meant,' said he, trying to reject the proffered coin; 'but no one shall take me into the Apostle cellar on the night of the first of September, not for love or money!'

THE CELLAR OF BACCHUS

'Stuff and nonsense! What do you mean?' 'I mean that it's an uncanny thing to go in there on Frau Rosa's own birthday.' I laughed till the vault rang. 'I've heard of a good many ghosts before now, but never heard of a wine-ghost: fancy an old man like you believing such tales: but I tell you, friend, I am serious. I have permission from their High Mightinesses to drink in the cellar tonight, time and place at my own discretion; and in their name I order you to lead me to the cellar of Bacchus.' This finished him. Unwillingly, but without answering, he took the taper and beckoned me to follow. We went first back through the great vault, then through a number of smaller ones, till our path came to an end in a narrow passage. Our steps echoed weirdly in the hollow way, and our very breath as it struck on the walls sounded like distant whisperings. At last we stood before a door, the keys rattled, with a groan the hinge opened, and the light of the candles streamed into the vault. Opposite me sat friend Bacchus on a mighty cask of wine: not slender and delicate like a Grecian youth had the cunning old wood carvers of Bremen made him; no, nor a drunken old sot with goggle eyes and hanging tongue, as vulgar mythology now and then blasphemously represents him (scandalous anthropomorphism I call it!). Because some of his priests, grown grey in his service, have gone about like that; because their bodies may have swelled full of good humour, and their noses been coloured by the burning reflection of the dark red flood; because their eyes may have become fixed through being constantly turned upwards in silent rapture,—are we to ascribe to the god the qualities of his servants? The men of Bremen thought differently. How cheerily and gaily the old boy rides on his cask: the round blooming face, the little bright eyes that looked down so wisely and yet so mockingly, the wide laughing mouth that has been the grave of so many a cask, the whole body overflowing with comfortable good living. It was his arms and legs, however, that specially delighted me. I almost expected to see him snap his chubby fingers, and hear his voice sing out a gay hurrah! Why, he looked as if at any moment he might jump off his seat and trundle his cask round the cellar, till the Rose and the Apostles joined in the merry dance, and chased each other round whooping. 'Merciful powers,' cried the cellarmaster, clinging tightly to me, 'I saw his eye roll and his feet move!' 'Peace, you old fool!' said I, feeling however rather queer, and looking anxiously at the wine god; 'it's only the dancing reflection of your taper. Well, we'll go on to the Apostle cellar, the samples will taste better there.' But as I followed the old man out of Bacchus' private room, I looked round, and the figure certainly seemed to nod his little head, and stretch out his legs, and give a shake as if from an inward giggle. One ascends from Bacchus to a smaller vault, the subterranean celestial firmament I called it, the seat of blessedness, where dwell the twelve mighty casks, each called after an apostle. What funeral vault of a royal race can compare with such a catacomb as this? Pile coffin on coffin, trim the everlasting lamps that burn before the ashes of the mighty dead, let black-on-white marble speak in epigrammatic phrase the virtues of the departed: take your garrulous cicerone with his crape-trimmed hat and cloak, listen to his praises of Prince This, who fell at the battle of That, and of Princess Tother on whose tomb the virgin myrtle is intertwined with the half-opened rosebud; see and drink in all the associations of such a place; but will it move you like this? Here sleeps, and has slept for a century, the noblest race of all. Dark-brown their coffins, and all unadorned—no tinsel, no lying epitaphs, simply their names inscribed on each in large plain letters, as I could see when the old fellow placed the taper on them. ANDREW, JOHN, JUDAS, PETER, and here on the right PAUL, on the left JAMES, good James. Paul is Nierstein of 1718, and James Rüdesheim, ye gods! Rüdesheim of 1726!

Ask not of their virtues; no one has any right to ask: like dark-red gold their blood sparkles in my glass; when it was first ripened on the hills of St. John it was pale and blonde, but a century has coloured it. What a bouquet! quite beyond the power of words to express. Take all the scents from all the flowers and trees, and all the spices of Araby and Ind, fill the cool cellar with ambergris, and let the amber itself be dissolved into fumes—and the result will be but poor and scentless compared to the liquid sunshine of Bingen and Laubenheim, of Nierenstein and Johannisberg. 'Why do you shake your head?' said I to my companion at last; 'you've no reason to be ashamed of these old fellows here. Come, fill your glass and here's good luck to the whole Twelve of them!'

'Heaven forbid that I should do anything of the kind,' he replied; 'it's an uncanny toast and an uncanny night for it. Taste them, sir, and let's pass on, I shiver in their presence.' 'Good-night, then, gentlemen—remember that I am everywhere and for ever at your service, most noble Lords of the Rhine.' 'Surely,' said the old fellow, 'those few drops haven't made you so drunk that you would raise the whole crew of sprites already? If you talk like that again I shall be off, though I should get the sack for it: I tell you that on this night the spirits imprisoned in these casks rise and hold infernal carnival here in this very spot, aye, and other spirits besides! I wouldn't be here after twelve o'clock for worlds.' 'Well, I'll be quiet, you old driveller, if you'll only take me on to my Lady Rose's apartment itself.' At last we reached it, the little garden of the queen of flowers. There she lay in all her majestic girth, the biggest cask I ever saw in my life, and every glass worth a golden guinea. Frau Rosa was born in 1615. Ah, where are the hands that planted her parent vine? where are the eyes that watched the ripening clusters? where the sun-browned feet that hurried to the festival when she was pressed in the sunny Rheingau, and streamed a pale gold rivulet into the vat? Like the waves of the stream that lapped the base of her cradle, they are gone no one knows whither. And where are their High-Mightinesses of the Hansa, who ruled when the Hansa was a League indeed, those worthy senators of Bremen who brought the blushing maiden to this cool grot for the edification of their grandchildren? Gone too—with two centuries over their heads, and we can only pour wine on their tombs.

Good luck to you, departed High-Mightinesses, and good luck to your living representatives, who have so courteously extended such hospitality to a Southerner! 'And goodnight to you, my Lady Rose,' added the old servant more kindly. 'Come along, sir, we can get out this way without going back, mind you don't stumble over the casks.' 'My good man, you don't imagine I'm going away, do you?' I replied. 'I have only just begun my night. Bring me some of that special '22, two or three bottles, into that big room behind there. I saw that wine growing green and saw it pressed, and now I'm going to prove to my palate that we can still grow something worth drinking.' The old boy expostulated, entreated, threatened, swore nothing should induce him to stay;—who wanted him to stay? Swore he daredn't leave me here;—did he think I was going to carry off Frau Rosa in my arms? Finally he agreed to let me remain if he might padlock me into the big room, and come at six o'clock tomorrow to wake me and receive his reward. Then, with a heavy heart, he put three bottles of the '22 on the table, wiped the glass, poured me out a little, and wished me good-night, double-locking and padlocking the door

14

behind me, more apparently out of tender anxiety for me than out of fear for his cellar. The clock struck half-past eleven as I heard him say a prayer and hurry away. When he shut the outer door of the vaults at the top of the stairs, there was an echo like the thunder of cannons through the halls and passages.

So now I was alone keeping Retreat with my soul down in the bosom of the earth. Slumber above me and slumber around me, for the spirits of the dead are asleep by my side. I wonder if they dream of their brief childhood on the distant mountains, and the nightly lullabys sung to them by old Father Rhine; or the kisses of their tender mother the sun when they first opened their eyes in the bright spring air, of their first leafy garments which reflected themselves in their old Father's eyes.

Ah! my soul, I too have rosy days of youth to look back upon, spent upon the soft vine-clad hills and by the blue rivers of my native Swabia; ah the days and the day dreams of glory! What games, what picture-books, what mother-love, what gigantic Easter eggs, what armies of tin and paper! And then, my soul, think of the first little trousers and collars in which your mortal covering, so proud of its size, was dressed; think how your father gave you rides on his knee, and your grandfather lent you his long bamboo cane with a golden head to use as a hobby horse.

Another glass! And then look on a few years. Do you remember the sad morning when you were taken to see all the mournful solemnities of grandfather's funeral? Ah! what would you not have given to get him back. Peace, 'tis but for awhile that he slumbers. And then the delightful hours in the old library filled with folios that were evidently bound in leather for no other purpose than that of forming huts to protect you and your imaginary sheep and cattle from the imaginary rain. How roughly you treated the Higher Literature of your native land. Why, I remember throwing a quarto Lessing at my brother's head, for which he beat me unmercifully with 'Sophy's Journey from Memel to Saxony.' Rise too, ye walls of the old castle, with your half-ruined passage, your cellar, your gate, your courtyard, all of which served only as a playground for a squad of boys; soldiers and robbers, nomads and caravans we were. I didn't much care whether I represented Platoff or a Cossack trooper, Napoleon or Napoleon's charger. Scattered all over the world, in every rank of life, and the sport of every kind of fortune is now the little knot of boys who were the companions of my childhood; and you and I, my dear soul, being alone too erratic to turn soldier, chamberlain, artisan, or parson, have become that remarkable thing called Doctor of Philosophy, having had just sufficient brains between us to write a dissertation. Brains enough to find our way into the Bremen cellars, however.

Another glass! Sure there's an affinity between wine and the tongue. It goes quite straight till it comes to the throat; here, however, is set up a finger-post, directing 'To the Stomach' and 'To the Head.' The latter is the path of the nobler particles of the grape-juice; the pure spirits that inhabit it will ever soar, and sensible, peaceful people they are for the most part, if there are not too many of them there together; but you know the best philosophers will quarrel when half a dozen of them of different intellectual complexions are closely packed in a small room.

How fair is that fourth period of life, (which we begin with the fourth glass.) Fourteen years old, my soul; but the boyish games are left behind, and you are steeped to the lips in reading—especially Goethe and Schiller, over whom you pore without understanding much. You think, however, you understand it all, and you have already kissed Elvira behind the cupboard door, and broken Emma's heart. Perjured villain! she may be another Charlotte, and she may possibly even have read some of Clauren, and be deeply in love with thee (and him). Let the scene change. I blow a greeting to that dear Alpine valley [Blaubeuern] where I spent so many years at school; the cloister roof, the walks over the brasses of dead abbots, the church with the wonderful high altar, the images dipped in the bright gold of sunrise. Thanks be to the strong Alpine air that I was ever full fledged and can fly as well as most people.

Another glass! Another period. That is a better glass than the last, I think—there's an aroma about it that the other lacked. And what a period that was! My college days! High, noble, savage, inharmonious, rough, fair; all opposites and contrasts that ever existed, blended then. No outsider can ever know the delights, and an outsider can hardly choose but laugh at the follies. Mixed with all the dross we bring up from thence there are generally some particles of fine gold. The music of our life would be strange indeed to one who had not sung and laughed with us. I know well what my granddad felt when he crossed the name of some fellow-collegian in his Book of Memory. God bless them all!

Another glass, by the immortal gods, and another bottle this time! From Friendship to Love. The most wonderful thing of this period (period six, please observe, my soul) was that its grades fitted themselves into and took their colour from my reading. Especially my affections got coloured from Wilhelm Meister; that is to say, I hardly knew whether it was Emmeline or the gentle Camilla, or even Ottilie. Didn't all three peep out from behind jalousies in bewitching nightcaps to hear the mournful squeaks which my numbed fingers elicited from the guitar? And when all three proved but heartless coquettes, I swore I would never marry till I was forty. Yet the little god slides from the eyes of the loved one into the heart of the victim. For am I not a victim? Is not she the coldest listener of all when I sing? did she ever vouchsafe me a single glance of encouragement? As I am not a general officer, I can't get mentioned in a despatch as having eight bullets in my breast and 'lying in a precarious condition,' even if we were not at peace. If I was only a drummer I could go and make a disgusting noise under her window till she was obliged to look out to tell me to go away, and I would then descend from fortissimo to piano and adagio, for I suppose one could do adagio even upon a drum. But the only fame she is likely to hear of me is that some one will tell her to-morrow that I boozed in the Town Cellar from midnight to six a. m.

Now is no one awake but the highest and the lowest in the town,—the watchman on the top of the cathedral tower, and I deep down in the bowels of the earth. If I were the watchman I would be singing to a certainty, so I don't see why I should not wake the echoes down here. *She* won't hear either of us, so here goes.

When at the lonely midnight hour
I pace my rounds upon the tower,
I muse upon my love afar,
Whose troth is fixed as morning star.
When to the flag at honour's call
I flew, her kiss was worth it all;
She decked my hat with ribbands blue,
Then pressed me to her heart anew.
And still her love's as warm as then,
It gives my hand the strength of ten;
It lends my heart a firmer beat,
To think in absence on my Sweet.
E'en now within her room she kneels
And wings to Heaven her dear appeals,
All lonely by the pale lamp's ray,
For one she loves that's far away.
But if my danger haunt thy breast,
Yet dry thy tears, and be at rest;
I stand in God's own armour clad,
He loves an honest soldier lad.
The clocks ring out, the round is near.
My hour of rest will soon be here;
Sleep rock thy brain, and set it free
To dream, and only dream of me.

Midnight! and is she dreaming of me? It always seems to me as if at this mysterious hour the earth gave a little tremble, and the dead who sleep in her bosom turned in their heavy slumber as if to mutter a prayer of *Domine quousque*? That distant bell is borne to me very differently from the 'twelve great shocks of shameless noon.' Hark! did not a door shut in one of the further vaults? Strange, if I didn't *know* that I was perfectly alone here I should believe that I heard footsteps. Yes, there are footsteps, and now they

18

are at my door too. Never mind, the door's well locked; no mortal can disturb me. *No mortal*; yet the door flies open!...

Two men stood there, making fantastic compliment of yielding the *pas* to each other. One was tall and haggard, with a long black wig, a dark red coat made by some old French tailor, and covered with gold tassels and gilt buttons. His immensely long thin legs were clad in tight trousers of black velvet, with gold knee-buckles; he had stuck his sword with its porcelain handle through his breeches pocket; when he bowed he flourished a three-cornered hat, and the curls of his peruke rustled down his shoulders like a waterfall. He had a pale face, sunken eyes, and a fiery red nose. The little fellow to whom he wished to yield precedence was quite different. His hair was plastered down with white of egg and then twisted into two long rolls like pistol holsters at the sides—and a plait about a yard long hung down his back. He wore a little steel-grey coat faced with red, and, beneath that, great riding boots, and a richly embroidered waistcoat which covered his plump figure to the knee, and a huge sword was fastened to his side. There was something good-tempered in his face, especially the eyes. He too performed wondrous evolutions with a huge beaver hat. I recovered a little from my terror while their courtesy proceeded to the verge of absurdity: at last they settled it by opening the other half of the door and marching in arm-in-arm. They hung their hats on the wall, unfastened their swords, and sat down silently without noticing me: I think I disliked their silence even more than anything else. Before however I had mustered courage to break it, more steps were heard, and four other gentlemen entered, dressed in somewhat similar fashion: one of them for the chase apparently. 'Greeting, gentlemen of the Rhine! it's long since we met,' said the pale-faced man with the red nose. 'Greeting, greeting, Mr. James, Mr. Matthew, greeting Mr. Judas. But what's this? where are the glasses and the pipes, where's the tobacco? Has that old fool not waked out of his sinful snoring yet? I suppose he is still in Our Lady's churchyard; but stay, I'll ring him up'—and he seized a great bell that stood on the table and rang it till the halls re-echoed. The three new comers took their seats at the table, and sat silent after the first greeting, especially one whom they called Andrew, who sat between the huntsman and the red-nosed man; he was evidently a person nice of his manners and appearance, his features were still youthful, and a gentle smile played upon his lips. There were varieties in the dress and expression of all, but not such as to have particularly fastened themselves upon my remembrance. As it usually is with old drinkers, conversation flagged for want of liquor; until, in answer to the summons of the bell, a new figure appeared at the door—a piteous-looking old man with trembling legs and grey hair, with a sort of death's-head face. With much exertion he dragged forward a great basket, and greeted the guests humbly.

'Hurrah,' they cried, 'here's Balthasar, slip along old fellow, on with your glasses and pipes; what a time you have been!'

THE GENTLEMEN OF THE RHINE

The old man gave a rude yawn, and declared that he had almost overslept the first of September: 'I sleep so sound, d'ye see, since they've new paved the churchyard, that I'm getting to hear rather badly. But here's only six of you yet, and where's my Lady Rose?' 'Just you put on the bottles, old chap, and then you may go across and rattle your dry bones against their casks, and tell them it's time to get up,' cried one of them; but the words were hardly spoken when a great noise and laughter was heard. 'Rosa, Rose, Lady Rose, hurrah, hurrah for Bacchus, hurrah for Rosa!' The ghostly companions within shouted with delight to the same effect, and clinked their glasses to the health of the Rose. Balthasar threw his cap up to the ceiling in his joy. In they came: Bacchus, my old friend who had bestrid the cask, had got down off it—not a rag of clothing on him—yet in he came, leading his blushing Rose, an ancient matron of stately mien and considerable stoutness of figure: splendidly dressed, too, she was like a true old Rhineland lady. Time might have written a few wrinkles on her brow and mouth, the fresh colour of youth might be a trifle wanting on her cheeks, but two hundred years had but added dignity to her contour. What though her eyebrows had grown grey, and there were— hush, yes there were really—a few ugly grey hairs on her chin, her locks

20

above were nut-brown, with but very slight tinge of silver here and there. Her head was covered with a black velvet cap, fitting close to her temples: her jacket was of the finest cloth, and the red velvet bodice that peeped from beneath it was laced with silver hooks and chains. Necklace, a string of garnets and gold coins. Her skirt was of thickly pleated brown cloth, and she wore a sort of toy white apron, with a huge leather pocket at one side and a bunch of huge keys at the other. In short, she was the very picture of a worthy matron of Mainz or Coblentz, of the years immediately preceding the Thirty Years War. Six jolly companions followed her, dressed in the same fashion as my friends who were already seated, and all with their wigs somewhat awry. How politely Bacchus led his lady-love to the table! how politely she bowed to the company as she sat down! As for her fat little sweetheart, Balthasar had to put a great pillow under him, or he would not have been able to get his nose above the table. When all were seated I realised that they were indeed the spirits of those mighty Rhinewines that I had tasted an hour before; the twelve Apostle-casks, Bacchus and the old Rose.

'Well, well, it's a long while since 1700, Mistress Rose,' said one of them, 'but we seem to be all in pretty good condition, and I vow you are as young and handsome as ever. Here's good luck and long life to your sweetheart and yourself, my dear.' 'Rosa, Frau Rosa, the Rose, long life and health to her!' shouted all, and Bacchus tossed off two quarts at a gulp, which had the visible effect of making him look more like an inflated bladder than ever.

'Thank you, most honoured apostles and cousins,' said she, bowing graciously; 'but when you refer to my sweetheart I don't know whom you mean; you confuse a modest maiden.' The modest maiden sought refuge in a mighty draught of wine. 'Sweetheart,' said Bacchus, looking tenderly at her and pressing her hand, 'be not coy, sweetheart; you know well whose heart has been yours any time these 200 vintages; and I don't mind proving it to you by this chaste salute'—and he bent forward to kiss her. 'If all these young people were not here,' she murmured—but amid shouts of laughter from the young people she allowed him to take his due by force and with interest. Then he tossed off a bowl or two and began to sing in a rich mellow voice:

There's not a palace in the land

So fair as this of Bremen,

Its spacious floors, its halls so grand

A king would feel no shame in:

And sure 'tis decked with everything

To take the fancy of a king;

But the thing that best would win it
Is the Lady fair within it.
Her eyes like sparkling Rhenish shine,
Her cheeks are bright as roses,
Her heavy draperies rich and fine
Are decked with fragrant posies:
Of heart-of-oak her farthingale,
Her girdle of the birchwood pale,
And her bodice trim she faces
With iron clasps and laces.
But ah, her bedroom too is barred
With locks and bolts of iron,
She slumbers soft nor dreams how hard
The threshold 'tis to lie on.
I knock in vain from twelve to four,
Arise, my love, and ope the door
That bars thy chamber cosy,
Come forth, my lovely Rosie!
So pass I every midnight hour
Before her lonely dwelling,
Once, only once, and never more,
The fairy lass was willing.
And since I drew that honeyed kiss
My heart's been drunken all with bliss—
Ah, just once more, my treasure,
Fill me a brimming measure!

'That's enough of such indelicate allusions, now, Mr. Bacchus,' says she; 'you know very well that their High Mightinesses keep me strictly locked up, and don't allow me to admit anyone at all.' 'Not even me, dear Rosie,' said he; 'ah, I think they would wink at it if you let me in now and then for a taste at your lips.' 'You're a rogue,' she answered, 'and little better than a Turk. I should like to know how many sweethearts you want. I know of your goings on with those frivolous French girls, Miss Champagne, (who has no more colour in her face than a dried pea,) and Fräulein von Bordeaux, the sickly minx. Ah, you have not the true Rhinelander's heart, nor understand the Rhinelander's love.' 'Pooh, my dear,' says he, 'I have visited these ladies occasionally, and amused myself with their wit, but nothing else; rest assured, my dearest, my heart is thine alone.' 'And then I fancy,' she went on, 'that I have heard some stories from Spain. Of poor Lady Xeres I will say nothing, (that's too well-known a story for you to deny); but how about the Señorina Dentilla di Rosa, Señorina San Lucar, and Señora Ximenes—a married lady too?' 'You carry your jealousy too far,' said he, with some asperity. 'I don't see why one should give up one's old connexions. As for the Señora Ximenes, I merely visit her out of kindness to you as being your relation.' 'Our relation?' muttered Rosa and the others, 'how's that?' 'Don't you know,' he continued, 'that she is originally from the Rhine? The most excellent hidalgo, Don Ximenes, took her from thence to his home in Spain when she was a very tender maid, and there she settled, and naturally took his family name. But she preserves with the Spanish sweetness much of the true German character, especially in colour and scent.' 'Long life to her, then,' cried they all, 'if she really is Rosie's cousin.' Rosa did not seem quite satisfied with her sweetheart's cunning mode of extricating himself from the scrape, so she changed the subject by turning round to the others and rallying them each in turn on the way in which the years had treated or spared them. One looked pale, she said, another was but half awake, a third had grown fat, almost too lazy to drink, a fourth was as ready for a joke as ever, and so on—'but hallo, why there are thirteen of you. Who's that in the strange clothing over there? who brought him in?'

Was I frightened or not? None of them looked pleased at my presence: but I said, 'I present my compliments to this worthy assemblage; I am really nothing but a man, who has taken a degree of Ph.D., and at present my residence is at the Frankfurt hotel in this city.'

'But, oh man who hast taken a degree, how camest thou here, man?' 'Apostle,' I answered—it was Peter whose eyes flashed fire on me as he spoke—'I'll trouble you not to call me man till we're better acquainted. And as for this society into which you say I have come, you are quite in error; it came to me, not I to it, for I had been sitting in this very room nearly an hour past' (I don't know whence I got the courage to say this—probably from the 'Special '22'). 'But what were you doing in the cellar at this time of night, sir?' said Bacchus rather more gently; 'you ought to be asleep.' 'Your Honour,' says I, 'I had excellent reasons for being here. I am a particular friend of the noble drink that is stored here, and, by favour of the not less noble Senate, I received permission to pay you all a visit—time and place not specified.'

'So you like to drink Rhine wine,' said Bacchus; 'that's a good liking to have in these days, when most men have grown so cold towards the golden spring,' 'Yes,' growled out the man in the red coat, 'no one will drink us now except here and there a travelling doctor, like this fellow, or a schoolmaster out for a holiday; and most of them water it first.' 'I beg most respectfully to contradict you, Mr. Jude,' said I. 'I have already tried you all round, and had but recently sat down to a few modest bottles of a more contemporaneous vintage, and that I have paid for myself.' 'Don't get hot, doctor,' said my Lady Rose, 'he didn't mean to hurt your feelings; he only reflected upon the low manners and bad taste of the present day.' 'Bad taste, low manners, I should think so,' said another. 'The generation that concocts a detestable mixture of brandy and half a dozen kinds of syrups, and calls it Château Margaux or Sillery, must indeed feel itself unworthy of a noble drink. And then people wonder why they get red rings round their mouths and a splitting headache the next day. Cochineal and brandy, nothing else!'

'What a life it was too when we were young, even as late as '26; yes, even as late as '50. Every evening, were it bright sunshiny spring, or deep wintry snow, the little rooms here were alive with joyous guests. The Senators of Bremen sat with majestic wigs on their heads, their weapons at their sides, and their glasses before them. That's what I call honour and dignity. Here, here, not *upon* the earth was their council chamber; here the true hall of the senate; here was settled over the cool wine the affairs of the nation and of most other nations besides. If they didn't agree they never quarrelled, but just drank each other's healths till they did; and if they ever failed it was because they didn't go on drinking long enough—but this rarely happened. Equal friends of the noble wine, how could they but be friends of each other? And on the next day their word pledged overnight was held sacred, and the resolves taken overnight were executed coolly enough in the morning.'

'Ah, the good old times,' said another Apostle, 'and it is still, you know, a custom that every Councillor keeps a little wine-book or drinking account, reckoned up and discharged at the end of the year. When a man sat here every night of his life, he didn't care to be always putting his hands in his pockets, so it was worked on the tally system, and I hear there are still a few brave old fellows left who use the same plan.'

'Yes, yes, children,' said the old Rose, 'it was another world a couple of centuries, or even one, or even half a century ago. They used to bring their wives and daughters into the cellar with them, and the fair Bremen maids, who were famed far and wide for bright eyes and rosy cheeks and voluptuous lips, drank nothing but good Rhine wine. Now forsooth, they must have tea and stuff like that, wretched foreign stuff, which girls in my time would only take if they had a little cough or sore throat, as a drug. And will you believe me, people actually put sweet Spanish stuff into true Rhine wines because they say we are sour.'

The Apostles roared with laughter at this last idea, and I couldn't help joining. As for Bacchus, he had to be patted on the back by Balthasar to recover him. 'Yes, the g-g-g-good old times,' sputtered he as he got breath again, 'every burgher drank his honest half gallon and went home as sober as a judge: now a glass upsets them, they're so out of practice.'

'There was a fine story to that effect a couple of centuries ago,' said my Lady, and smiled to herself at the recollection of it. 'Please tell it us, Frau Rose. Yes! the story! the story!' they all began to cry. She emptied her bowl to clear her voice, and began.

'You must know that in 1620 or 30 there was a great rumpus in Germany about a very small matter—the Form of Religion. Each side wanted its own form shoved down the throat of the other, and instead of sitting down to talk it over sensibly over a pipe of wine, they proceeded to knock each other on the head. Albrecht von Wallenstein, the Kaiser's field-marshal in particular, made sad havoc of the Protestant countries, until the King of Sweden, called Gustavus Adolphus, took pity on them, and crossed the Baltic with a large army, and went at it hammer and tongs in defence of the Protestant religion. Well, they fought a lot of battles, and chased each other about from the Rhine to the Danube, and from the Danube to the Rhine with mighty little result. At that time Bremen and the other Hanse towns were neutral, and did not wish to quarrel with either party; but as Gustavus wanted a passage through their territories, he determined to send an embassy to them. It was well known, however, that everything like state business in Bremen was transacted in this cellar, and that the Bremeners were good hands at stowing away liquor: so the king was in some perplexity lest his ambassadors should be drunk under the table, and then made to sign an unfavourable treaty. Now, there was by chance in the Swedish camp a captain of the Yellow Regiment who was a notable drinker. Two or three quarts for breakfast were a trifle to him, and in the evening he would half empty a four-gallon cask and sleep well after it. The chancellor Oxenstiern brought this man to the king's notice. Captain Tosspot he was called. The king was much pleased when he observed his nose, which was of the right copper hue, and asked him how much he *could* drink if it was a case of life and death. "O king," he answered,

"I am but a poor captain, and wine is very dear. I never tried seriously. I can't afford to exceed my seven quarts a day; but if your majesty would stand treat I would undertake to finish twelve at least. But my squire who is called Balthasar the Bottomless, is a much harder drinker than I am." Balthasar was called, a thin, ashy-pale little fellow with lank straight hair, and the king sent them into a tent by themselves, with some fine old casks of Hochheimer and Nierstein, and told them to get drunk. They began at 11 a.m., and by 4 p.m. they had finished eight gallons of Hochheimer and twelve of Nierstein. When the king went to see them they were quite sober, but Captain Tosspot said he thought he should soon have to loosen his sword-belt, and Balthasar had undone three buttons of his collar. Then said the king, "What better ambassadors can I find to talk the fair city of Bremen into its senses?" So Tosspot was made ambassador and Balthasar the Bottomless his secretary, and they were properly rigged out, and their instructions were made out; and the first of these was that they were to drink nothing but water on the way to Bremen, that the battle in the cellar might be more glorious afterwards; another was that Tosspot was to rub his nose with a white ointment, that no one might see what a practised mouth he was. They arrived safely at Bremen, but both of them naturally quite ill through drinking water: the Senators of Bremen thought they would have an easy victory over two such milksops, and so the burgomaster said he would look after the ambassador, and Dr. Redpepper should settle the secretary. So in the evening they were solemnly led into the cellar with a lot of senators who were invited to assist in the negotiations. They sat down in this room and had a little spiced meat and ham and red herrings; but when Mr. Ambassador Tosspot wanted to begin the negotiation in an honourable manner, and Mr. Secretary Balthasar took parchment and ink-horn from his pocket, "Not so, noble gentlemen," said the burgomaster; "it is not the custom in Bremen that we should settle weighty matters with a dry throat, we will first drink to one another, as our ancestors in like cases have always done." "I am but a poor drinker," said the captain, "but if it so pleases your High-Mightiness I will take a drop." So they began to drink and treat at the same time; and to encourage their guests, the senators and the doctor and the burgomaster went a little further than usual with the Rüdesheimer. At each new bottle the strangers excused themselves, assuring the burgomaster that it was beginning to get into their heads; which of course delighted him immensely: and at last said the burgomaster, "now for bishnesh." But as the "bishnesh" went on, the burgomaster went to sleep while he was defining the word neutrality, and Doctor Redpepper lay already under the table: then the other senators came and went on with the negotiations and the drinking; but the captain, who kept five men running backwards and forwards filling his glass for him, drank them all under the table.

'All—but one. Mr. Senator Walther was a man of whom ugly tales would infallibly have been told, if he had not been Mr. Senator. He was a man who had raised himself from a humble position in his craft-guild to be an alderman, and then to his present place. He was a very tall bony man. He alone now held out with the two guests, and put away twice as much as both of them. Moreover, he seemed as sensible as ever, whereas Tosspot was beginning to feel as if a wheel were going round in his head. But the curious thing was this, that when Walther drank a glass Balthasar fancied that he saw a thin blue mist rise and exude from his black hair. These two, however, drank bravely on till Tosspot dropped peacefully to sleep with his head pillowed against the burgomaster's arm.

'Then said the Senator to the Secretary, "My dear fellow, you drink wonderfully well, but I fancy you are more familiar with the bridle than the pen." Balthasar attempted some bluster about his Majesty's Embassy, but the other replied with a terrible laugh, "Ho, ho? and do secretaries in your country always wear such clothes and carry such pens?" Then the groom looked at his dress and saw with alarm that he had on his ordinary stable coat and had a curry comb in his hand. Bluer than ever looked the mist about Walther's head as he tossed off another quart. "Heaven forbid, sir," said poor Balthasar, "that I should drink with you any longer. I see you are a magician."

"True," said the man, "but we needn't go into that, most honourable horse-combing secretary; the point of the thing as far as you are concerned is, that it is no use your trying to drink me under the table, for I have a little tap screwed into my brain through which the fumes of the wine can evaporate." It was indeed true, and he inclined his head towards Balthasar to show him the process. The groom clapped his hands with delight: "That's a most excellent device, sir; couldn't you screw such a thing as that into my head? I will give you everything I possess for such an article." "No, that can't be done," said the other thoughtfully; "you are not learned either in magic or anything else; but as I have taken a great liking to you I will serve you with all my power. Listen: The post of cellarmaster is vacant here at present. Leave, oh Bottomless one, the Swedish service, where there is more water than wine, and come into the service of the most noble the Council of this City. Even if we do lose a few dozen casks of wine per annum, which you drink in secret, that won't matter, we have been long looking out for a fit person for the place. I will make you cellarmaster to-morrow if you like: whereas if you don't like, all the town shall know to-morrow that the Swede has sent us a groom as a secretary." This proposal tasted to Balthasar like a draught of good wine, he cast a glance into the immeasurable realm of drink that was already prospectively his, and accepted the offer at once. After this there remained several little points to be settled; as for instance, what was to be done with

27

Balthasar's soul when he ceased to be cellarmaster in the course of nature: all these were satisfactorily determined, and Captain Tosspot went back to the Swedish camp without his secretary, without his treaty, and with a bad headache. And when the Imperialists afterwards came to Bremen and occupied it, the burgomaster was right glad that he had not allied himself too closely with Gustavus.'

Thus the Rose, amid much laughter and thanks for her story; but one of us asked, 'And what became of Balthasar the Bottomless, did he remain in his new situation long?' Frau Rosa turned round laughing and pointed to a corner of the room, and said, 'There he sits still as the bold drinker sat 200 years ago!' There he sat sobbing between every draught of Rhenish that he drank, poor shrunken pallid fellow: it was the very same man who had come up so sleepily when the big bell was rung for him a while before. All were anxious to hear the conditions which had been wrung from him by Senator Walther respecting his soul. 'Oh sir,' he replied, in a voice which sounded as if Eternal Death was accompanying him on the bassoon, 'don't require me to tell you.' 'Out with it! what did he want? Out with it!' cried all. 'My soul.' 'What for?' 'For wine.' 'Speak plainly, old fellow, what did he do with your soul?' He was silent for a long time, and at last said, 'Why should I tell this, gentlemen? It is a dreadful thing, and you don't know what it is to lose a soul as none of you ever had one.' 'All the more reason why you shouldn't be afraid of hurting our feelings,' said another. 'But there is a mortal here, I may not say it before him.' 'Go on,' said I, trembling all over, 'I'm not easily shocked; after all, I suppose it was only the Devil who came for you, and he does that every night on the stage.' 'Well then,' said the old man, 'it was the man with the tap who had begun by selling *his* soul to the Devil, but on condition that he should redeem it if he could find a substitute. He had tried many but all had escaped him; so he made sure of me. I had grown up a wild youth with no teaching, and the wars had left me no time for thinking of my own soul, or Heaven, or Hell, and my only idea was to have a good time during my life. And my idea of a good time was plenty to drink and all day to drink it in. Walther perceived this, and says he, "To live and swill in this Vinous Paradise for two or three decades that would be a life, hey Balthasar? Wouldn't it?" "Ah!" said I, "I should think it would, but how could I attain such felicity?" "Which would you think most of, living here and drinking to your heart's content as long as you *do* live, or of the stories about what will happen afterwards?" I swore a dreadful oath, "My bones will go where so many of my comrades' bones are lying. When a man is dead he neither feels nor thinks. I have seen that plainly enough in the case of many a poor fellow whose skull has been smashed by a bullet; and therefore I will choose to live and be merry." "Very well," said he. "Then you renounce and forswear the hereafter, do you? then I can easily manage to make you cellarmaster here; only write your name in this book, and swear a binding oath at the same time." I swore again that the Devil or whoever else liked might have all that remained of me after death. When I had said this I was aware that we were no longer two, but a third sat by me and gave me the book to sign.' 'Who was it?' cried all the company. 'It was the Devil.' Weird words: even the spirits of the Vines looked gravely into their glasses, and Bacchus and Frau Rosa were pale and silent, and we heard only the old man's teeth chattering in his skull. 'Well! I *could* write,' he went on, 'and I wrote now just what was asked of me: and from that time my life went on in riot and merriment, and there was none so gay in Bremen as Balthasar the Bottomless. I drank up all that was oldest and most precious in the cellar. I never went to church, but when the bells rang I came down here and sat down by the best cask and let the tap run into my goblet. As I became old a creepy feeling would now and then come over me, but I drowned all thoughts of death in wine. I had no wife to lament and no children to comfort me: and so on and so on for long years till from very weakness I longed to rest in the grave. Then one day I felt as if I were awake and yet couldn't get up, my eyes wouldn't open, my fingers were stiff, my legs were like logs of wood, and I heard the people come to my bed side, and they felt me all over and said, "Old Balthasar is gone at last." This really frightened me. Dead and not asleep? Dead and still thinking? Though my heart had ceased to beat, something within me beat loudly enough.' 'Your soul, poor fellow,' they whispered. Balthasar nodded and went on. 'Then they measured my length and my breadth to make the six boards ready, and put me in with a hard cushion of shavings under my head and nailed up the coffin, and carried me out into our Lady's churchyard. I heard the bell tolling in the Cathedral, though no eye wept for me; and my soul was ever more frightened because I couldn't sleep. They had dug my grave. I can still hear the whistle of the rope which they drew up as I lay down below. Then they threw stones and earth on me, and it was silent all around me. But my soul grew more and more terrified as it drew towards evening. I knew a little prayer from old times, but my lips wouldn't move. I heard ten—eleven—strike, and at last TWELVE,—when a fearful blow resounded on my coffin'…. A blow that made the hall re-echo now burst open the door of the room, and a great white figure appeared on the threshold. By the wine and the horrors of the night, I had been so ecstasised as to be taken out of myself. I did not scream or jump up, but stared quietly at this new apparition of terror, and simply said, 'Well, I suppose this is the Devil.'

Have you realised the fearful moment in Don Giovanni, when heavy steps ring nearer and nearer, and Leporello comes back screaming and the statue of the governor stalks in to supper, as he was bidden? So this figure: gigantic, with measured echoing tread, a huge sword in hand, in full armour, but unhelmeted, it stalked into the room. It was of stone, yet the stony lips moved, and said, 'Greeting, dear vine-spirits from my beloved river: greeting to you on your birthday, fair child of my neighbour; greeting, My Lady Rose, may I take a seat in your assembly?'

All looked in amazement at the figure. But Rosa clapped her hands with joy, and cried, 'Why, it's Roland! the great stone Roland that has stood in the square at Bremen for ever so many years! This will indeed be a memorable night when you do us so much honour, sir. Put your shield and sword away, and make yourself comfortable. Will you take a seat by my side? Oh, how glad I am!'

The wooden Bacchus, who had been growing fatter and fatter all this time, cast discontented looks now at Roland and now at the Lady of his heart, who had expressed her pleasure so loudly and unrestrainedly. He murmured something about 'uninvited guests being a bore,' and stamped his legs impatiently. But my Lady appeased him with sweet looks and pressed his hand under the table. Room was made for Roland on her other side, and the latter laid down his spear and shield in a comer, and sat down rather awkwardly on a chair. But, alas! the chair was made for the cushioned forms of the burghers of Bremen town, not for a stone giant, and it at once cracked and fell in pieces under him, leaving him sprawling. 'Vile race of weaklings,' he cried, as he rose, 'that puts together such furniture as this, whereon in my time a tender lady could not have sat in safety!' But Balthasar rolled a huge cask up to the table, and persuaded the knight to try it; a couple of staves cracked, but the cask held firm. It was the same with his wine. The glass that Balthasar offered him he shivered to fragments as he grasped it. 'Well,' said the latter rather angrily, 'you might have taken off your stone gauntlets.' A silver goblet of the tumbler-shape holding about a quart escaped with a few unimportant dents, and the knight tossed off its contents.

'How do you like the liquor?' said Bacchus; 'it must be dry work up there on your pillar. I suppose you haven't tasted wine for years?'

'It is good, by my sword, very good. What growth is it?'

'Red Ingelheimer, noble sir,' said Balthasar.

The stony eyes of the knight took fire and sparkled as he heard this, a soft smile beautified his stern features, and he looked with affection into the goblet.

'Ah, dear beloved Ingelheim! how sweet it sounds! the noble castle of my knightly Kaiser. So, even in these days thy name is named! and the vines still bloom which Karl first planted by *his* Ingelheim! Do the men who live now ever speak of Roland? or of his great master?'

'That you must ask of the mortal here,' said Jude; 'he calls himself Doctor and Master of Arts, and he must give you an account of his race.' The giant turned his eyes inquiringly on me, and I said, 'Noble Paladin, mankind has indeed grown bad and careless of all that is great and lofty: its blind gaze is fixed upon the present, and looks neither before nor after. Yet so wretched are we not yet become, as to have wholly ceased to remember the glorious figures that once trod our native land; they still cast their shadow through the ages till it touches even us. Still are there hearts that fly for refuge to the memories of the past, when the present has become too stale and mean for reflection. Still are there pulses which beat higher at the naming of mighty names, still men who wander with reverence through the ruins where sat the first German Kaiser on his throne with his Paladins and his bards around him. Karl and Oliver, Eginhard and the lovely Emma are still familiar in men's mouths. And where Karl is renowned there too is Roland unforgotten. Next to him thou stoodst in life, and next to him thou wilt stand in song and saga and history till Memory itself shall be no more. The final blast of thy warhorn still echoes in the hills of Roncesvalles, and will echo and echo on till it fades into the blare of the Latest Trumpet.' 'Not in vain, my Kaiser, not in vain have we lived! There *is* a posterity which does honour to our name,' cried the knight. 'True,' cried Frau Rosa, 'these men would deserve to drink the water of the Rhine instead of the vine blossom of its hills if they could forget the name of the man who first planted us in the Rheingau. My dear friends and apostles, up! a health to our glorious founder and ancestor! to Kaiser Karl, to Kaiser Karl!' The glasses rang again; but Bacchus said, 'Yes, it was a beautiful and a glorious time, and I rejoice in it as I did a thousand years ago. Where now there is one long wonderful garden from the shore of the stream to the tops of the hills, where grape climbs after grape up and down the terraces, there was nothing but wild dark forest before he came. Then he looked down from the mountains from his castle at Ingelheim, and he saw how even in March the sun greeted the hills so warmly as the snow slid down them into the stream; saw how early the trees became leafy there, and how tender and fresh the young grass looked as it burst upwards from the earth in the spring. And then there awakened in him the thought of planting vines where the wood grew. And a busy life began to move in the Rheingau beside Ingelheim; the wood vanished, and the earth was cleared to receive the vine. Then Karl sent men to Hungary and Spain, to Italy and Burgundy, to Champagne and Lothringen, and had vines brought from thence, and entrusted the cuttings to dear mother earth. And my heart rejoiced that he should extend my kingdom beside the noble stream of Germany, and when the first shoots blossomed there I came with all my train, and we camped upon the hills, and we worked in the earth, and we worked in the air, and we spread out delicate nets and caught the dews of spring lest they should fall too heavily; and we rose up and caught the rays of the sunshine, and poured them round the little swelling clusters, and we dived down and brought up water from the green Rhine for the roots, and water for the leaves. And when in autumn the first tender child of the Rheingau lay in its cradle we kept a great feast, and invited all the elements to celebrate it; and each came with some costly gift for the child. Fire laid his hand upon its eyes and said, "Thou shalt bear my sign upon thee for ever—there shall be fire in thee, albeit of such purity and transparency, that thou shalt impart noble courage beyond all other juice of the grape." And Air came in her golden garment of gossamer, and laid her hand upon the child's forehead and blessed him. "Be thy colour as bright and delicate as the golden edge of morning light upon the hills, as the golden tresses of the fair women of the Rheingau." And Water ran past him, all rustling with silver, and bent towards the child, saying, "I will be ever near thy roots, that thou mayst bloom and be green and cover the banks of the Rhine." But when Earth came she kissed his mouth tenderly, and blew with her sweet breath upon him. "The perfumes of all my most delicate herbs, the honey of all my fairest flowers," she said, "have I collected as an offering for thee. The most precious spikenard or ambergris shall be coarse beside thy scent; and thy fairest daughter shall be named after the Queen of Flowers—the ROSE!" Thus spake the elements, and we rejoiced at their promised blessings, and we adorned the child with vine leaves, and sent him to the Kaiser in his castle at Ingelheim. And the Kaiser marvelled at the beauty of the child, and from that day he esteemed the vines of the Rhine among the most splendid of his treasures.'

We sat silent for a while when Bacchus had finished, until her Ladyship requested Andrew to favour us with an old melody, which he did with great ease and grace, by singing a simple old song of the fourteenth or fifteenth century. The words have escaped my memory, but the tune I remember still. This set us all off, even Frau Rosa herself, who sang a pretty little air of 1615 with a rather trembling voice, and Roland also growled out in deep bass a Frankish war hymn, of which I could distinguish little. I was obliged to bear my part, so I began bravely,

The Rhine! the Rhine! the garden of the vine!

Heaven bless the noble Rhine!

Along his bank the clustered grapes entwine,

And patriot hearts inspire to guard the Rhine!

When they heard the words they pressed nearer, and nodded to one another, and stretched out their necks as if wishful not to lose a word. I sang louder and louder for their encouragement. It was inspiration enough to be heard by such a company. The old Rose kept time with her head, and gently hummed the chorus, and the Apostles gazed at me with surprise and joy in their eyes. When I had finished, all were loud in praise of the poor Doctor of Philosophy. 'What a song!' cried Bacchus himself, 'how my heart opens to it, dear Doctor, was it composed in that head of yours that's crowned with academic honours?' 'No, indeed, your honour, the composer has long been dead; he was called Matthew Claudius.' 'He knew a good glass of wine when he came across it, I'll go bail,' said another. 'I don't know, sir,' said I, 'though I have no doubt of it; but another great mortal has said,

Good wine is a good familiar creature, if it be well used,

and I think old Claudius had a similar idea, or he would never have written such a beautiful song, which all men still sing as they sit beneath the vine-covered arbours of the Rhine.' 'Well, Doctor,' said Bacchus, 'if they still sing songs like that they can't be quite such a miserable lot of fellows as you made out.'

'Ah, sir,' said I, 'your poetical "high soul" won't sin by allowing such a song to be poetry at all, just as your pietist finds the Lord's Prayer too simple and straightforward for him.' 'There have been fools in every age, sir,' said another, 'and every one is bound to clean the pavement opposite his own door only; but as we are upon the subject of the present times, tell us what has happened this year on the earth.'

'If I thought it would interest the ladies and gentlemen—' 'Go on,' cried Roland, 'and as far as I am concerned you may begin 500 years back, for I see nothing from my pedestal but cigar-makers, vintners, priests, and old women, and they don't make history, or didn't in my days.'

'First of all then, concerning German Literature …'

'Stop for Heaven's sake, man! Do you think we are going to listen to trash like that?' cried Peter. 'Poetasters and public-house squabbles!'

I was startled. If these people were not interested by our magnificent literature, if Goethe had no charms for them, what was the use of speaking to them at all?

I tried again. 'It was only last autumn that the stage was—' Howls of laughter drowned my voice. 'We want facts, man, history and facts only; do you suppose we care who spins your comedies and who hisses them?'

'Ah, sir,' I replied, 'you're sadly out of fashion. So's History. We have in fact only the Diet at Frankfurt. Among our neighbours it's true there's occasionally something—for instance, the Jesuits are up again in France, and it looks uncommonly as if the Jacobins were up in Russia.' 'Stuff!' cried one, 'you mean vice versâ.' 'No, I don't.' 'Well, that's odd.' 'And is there no war?' 'Just a little firespitting going on in Greece against the Turks.' 'Ha!' cried the Paladin, smashing a few planks of the table with his stone fist, 'that is good! By my sword, that is good! I have been angry for centuries at the tameness of Christendom while Greece is in chains. You live, sir, in a fine time, and your race is nobler than I thought. I retract my previous vituperation. So the knights of France and Germany, of Spain and England have set out again as erst under Richard of the Lion-heart, to fight the infidel? The fleets of Genoa cover the Mediterranean? the Oriflamme is raised on high within sight of the towers of Stamboul, and the banner of Austria floats over the foremost ranks. Ha! in such a case I would fain bestride once more my steed; I would make Durendal, my good sword, flash the lightnings of death indeed, and would rouse with one blast of my horn every hero who sleeps within the bounds of Europe!'

'Noble knight,' I answered—and again I blushed for the age in which I lived—'times are changed. You would probably be imprisoned as a Jacobin demagogue under the present circumstances, for neither the banner of Hapsburg nor the Oriflamme, neither the Leopard of England nor the Lion of Spain are to the fore in the present conflict.'

'Who then is fighting against the Crescent, if not these?'

'Simply the Greeks themselves.'

'The Greeks?' cried another, 'is it possible? and what are the other powers about?' 'They have their ambassadors with the Porte.' 'Man, man,' said Roland, stiffer than ever with amazement, 'what are you saying? a Christian state fighting for its freedom and left to do it alone? Holy Virgin, what a world is this!' and he crushed the silver goblet as if it had been cardboard, so that the wine in it splashed up to the ceiling; then rising from the table took his sword and targe, and passed with clanking strides out of the chamber.

'Why, what a hot-headed fellow he is!' said the Rose, shaking her kerchief, which was splashed with his wine. 'Does the stony fool want to go a-campaigning again in his old age? If he were to show himself they would certainly make him a right-hand man in a company of Prussian Grenadiers, for he's tall enough.'

'Do not be hard on him, my Lady Rose,' said one of the company, 'for he has the right stuff in him, and he showed it on many a stricken field. If his Kaiser had wished it he would have fought a thousand Mussulmans single-handed.'

'Let him go,' said Bacchus; 'I'm glad he's gone; he bored me with his strong heroics: a fellow ten feet high is out of place here. He showed me no respect. We should never have been able to dance while he was here; his legs would have broken if he had tried.' 'To the dance! to the dance!' they all cried. The wine god beckoned to me. 'Do you understand music, Doctor?' 'A little.' 'Keep good time?' 'Oh yes, I keep good time.' 'Then take this little barrel and this cooper's stave, and sit down besides the Bottomless one there; he is our cellarmaster and cornet player, and you shall accompany him on the drum.' I did as I was bid, but if my drumming was rather unusual, Balthasar's cornet-playing was even more so. He held the iron spout of a large empty cask to his mouth like a clarionet. Two more sat near me with huge wine-funnels which they used as trumpets, waiting for the signal. Then began a fearful rumbling and hooting, all out of tune, to which Turkish music was nothing. Balthasar's instrument had but two notes, the key note and an horribly high falsetto. As for the trumpeters the sounds of grief and anguish which they drew from their funnels was like nothing but the wailing of a Triton on a conch.

Bacchus and his sweetheart paraded in the height of the fashion of 200 years ago. Frau Rosa held her skirt wide out with both hands, so that she looked more like a great wine cask than ever. She didn't move far from her place, but tripped a few steps up and down and back again, and kept bobbing with little curtsies. Her partner meanwhile spun round her like a top, snapping his fingers and crying Halloo!

'TO THE DANCE! TO THE DANCE!'

When at last he seemed tired he beckoned to two of the others, and whispered something to them, whereon they took off Mistress Rose's apron, (which Bacchus had tied round his own neck when he began to dance.) Then the others stood all round and grasped the edge of it. Ha! thought I, now old

Balthasar is going to be tossed in a blanket. I hope he won't break his head against the low roof. Then to my horror two of the biggest of them came forward and seized—me; Balthasar chuckled. Struggling was vain; they laid me on the sheet shouting with laughter. 'Only not too high, my noble patrons, or I shall break my head; remember it's not like your saintships' heads,' I cried. Up and down I went, first three, four, then five feet high. Suddenly they began to pull harder, and I flew up—up—and like a cloud the roof opened, and I flew up beyond the roof of the Council Hall, beyond even the Cathedral tower. 'Ah!' thought I, 'now it's all over with me, I shall infallibly be spiked on the weather-cock in coming down, or at least break a few arms or legs; and I know what Adelgunde thinks of a man with broken limbs. Adieu! my love! my life! Then I began to descend as swiftly through the air, through the Council Hall, through the vault, but I lighted not upon the cloth, but just upon a chair which toppled over backwards with me to the floor.

Stunned by the awful fall I lay long, but at length a headache and the coldness of the ground awoke me. Anxiously I examined my limbs, but found nothing broken. Daylight was faintly streaming in through a cellar grating; on the table a candle was flickering as it expired, and round the table in front of each chair a long-shaped bottle with a label on its neck. The company was gone! But whither and how?

Thoughtfully I walked round the long table. The sample bottles stood where each one had sat. Frau Rosa's at the head of the board. Surely it couldn't have been a dream? No, one does not dream so vividly—besides, my headache from that bump! But I had little time left for reflections. I heard keys rattling at the door—it opened slowly, and my old friend of the evening before came in wishing me good morning. 'It has just struck six, sir,' said he, 'and I have come as you desired to let you out. Well, how did you sleep?' 'As well as one can upon a chair—pretty fairly, thank you.' 'Sir,' cried he, anxiously examining me, 'something strange happened to you last night—you look disturbed and pale, and your voice trembles.' 'Nonsense,' said I, 'what could have happened to me? I am only sleepy.' 'I am not so blind as you think,' said he, 'and, besides, the night watchman came to me early this morning and told me that as he passed by the cellar between twelve and one last night he heard all kinds of riot and revelry within there.' 'Pure imagination,' said I, 'I'm given to talking loud, and even to singing, in my sleep sometimes.'

'Never again,' said he, 'do I leave a gentleman alone in the cellar at night. The Lord knows what awful things he has not heard and seen. I wish you a most respectful good morning, sir.'

'But the thing that best would win it

Is the Lady Fair within it.'

Remembering these words of the joyous Bacchus as being particularly applied to Bremen and to my own case, I hurried, after I had slept a few hours, to bid good morning to the lovely Adelgunde. But she received me with more than wonted coldness, and when I whispered some affectionate words to her she fairly laughed aloud, and turning her back said, 'Go, and have your sleep well out, sir, first.' A friend, who was sitting at the piano in another corner of the room, followed me as I turned away, and taking my hand said, 'Dear Brother, it is all over with your love for her—put all thoughts of it out of your head.' 'I could see as much,' I answered; and then, *sotto voce*, 'The Devil take every pretty pair of eyes and every rosy mouth in the world!' 'But tell me,' says my friend, 'is it true that you stayed the whole night drinking in the wine cellar?' 'Well, yes! but whose business is that?' 'Heaven knows how she heard it, for she has been crying all the morning, and vows you are a mere vulgar sot, and she will have no more to do with you.' 'Well,' said I, steeling myself, 'good then; that proves she can never have loved me. Give her my kind regards; farewell.'

I ran home quickly and resolved to quit Bremen at once. As I left the market-place that evening I gave old Roland's statue a friendly wave of the hand, and to the horror of my postillion, he nodded a parting greeting at me with his stone head. I threw a kiss to the old Council Hall and its happy cellars, and curling up in the comer of my chaise allowed the fancies of the night to pass once more before my eyes.

Lightning Source UK Ltd.
Milton Keynes UK
UKHW012209100820
367994UK00009B/1311

9 783752 377989